PENNY TALES

by Virginia Schone

illustrated by Paul Richer

Parents' Magazine Press

New York

For Dan

Text copyright © 1977 by Virginia Schone
Illustrations copyright © 1977 by Paul Richer
All rights reserved
Printed in the United States of America

Library of Congress Cataloging in Publication Data
Schone, Virginia.
    Penny Tales.
    CONTENTS: The cat that stretched.–Doris, the
brontosaurus.–When Mr. Snippen snipped sneezeweed.
[etc.]
    [1. Animals–Fiction. 2. Short stories] I. Richer,
Paul. II. Title.
PZ7.S374Pe   [E]   76-17827
ISBN 0-8193-0850-1   ISBN 0-8193-0851-X lib. bdg.

CONTENTS

THE CAT THAT STRETCHED

The cat stretched from the living room to the dining room.

Then she stretched again, from the living room to the dining room to the bedroom.

She stretched once more, from the living room to the dining room to the bedroom and out the window.

Said the cat, "I must remember not to nibble on that rubber plant."

1

ELMER'S ELEGANT JOB

Elmer was an elephant. Early every morning, Elmer ate eighty eggs. He also carefully washed each ear. He wanted to look and smell good.

Then Elmer would rush to his elegant job. He was an elevator operator. The elevator was an express, and Elmer knew exactly how to run it.

He pressed the button UP, and up the elevator rose. Not once did it groan as it lifted Elmer into the sky.

When the elevator reached the top, Elmer pressed the button DOWN, and down to the ground he zoomed.

Of course, with an elephant running the express, only one passenger could fit at a time. And that person had to ride on Elmer's back.

But there weren't many complaints. After all, it isn't often a person gets to ride an elephant *and* an elevator at the same time.

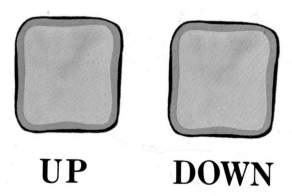

UP   **DOWN**

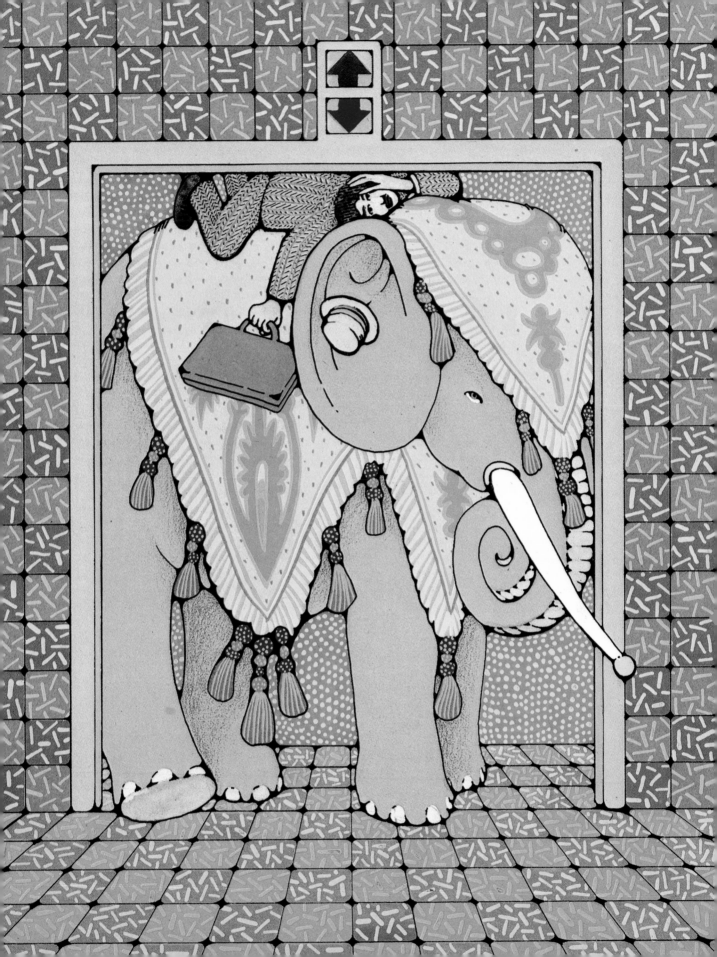

WHEN MR. SNIPPEN SNIPPED SNEEZEWEED

Mr. Snippen was snipping a snip of sneezeweed, when Mrs. Snippen said to Mr. Snippen, "Don't snip a snip of sneezeweed. Snip a snip of–of–AAAAAAAA–CHOOOOOO!"

Mrs. Snippen sneezed so hard, she sneezed herself into the next yard.

"I would stop snipping this sneezeweed," shouted Mr. Snippen to Mrs. Snippen, "and I would gladly snip a snip of achoo, if I knew where the achoo grows or what an achoo looks like."

Which just goes to show: giving clear directions is nothing to be sneezed at.

3

THE HONEY GUIDE AND THE BADGER

There was once a young bird called a honey guide. And one day, this young honey guide flew excitedly to a honey badger. "Come quick! I've found a beehive. You are strong. I need you to break it open."

"This is not a beehive," said the honey badger crossly, when he saw what the honey guide had found. "It's a kite, caught in a tree."

Another day, the honey guide flew to the badger again. "A beehive! Hurry!"

"Wrong again," grumbled the honey badger. "This time it's a balloon."

Not long afterward, the badger discovered the same young bird enjoying honey with another badger. "I put up with your mistakes," scolded the first badger. "Why didn't you call *me* when you found a real beehive?"

"You're such a grouch," said the young bird. "Why call you? You'd only spoil my fun."

4

THE OCTOPUS AND THE SNAIL

"Why are you crying," Snail asked Octopus, who sat weeping into eight handkerchiefs.

"I don't have a house like yours," said Octopus.

"Be glad," said Snail. "A house is a heavy burden."

Octopus continued to cry. "Now why are you crying?" asked Snail.

"The sun is so hot."

"Then dive into the water," said Snail.

Still Octopus sobbed. "What is it this time?" asked Snail.

"Just think of all the handkerchiefs I'll have to wash once I stop crying!" wailed Octopus.

"Some people can always find something to cry about," said Snail with a sigh, and she slipped back into her shell.

JENNY HENNY GETS A LETTER

Jenny Henny received this letter from her sister:
"Dear Jenny,
I need a new dress.
Please send one, quick!
Frannie."
Jenny Henny wrote this answer:
"Dear Frannie,
I need a new sister.
Please send one, quick!
Jenny."
But Jenny Henny sent the dress, too. Someone once told her that birds of a feather should stick together.

THE TINY TRAMP

Through the school window floated a dandelion going to seed. White tufts shot out everywhere. Hanging onto the dandelion as if it were an umbrella-parachute, was a tiny tramp. He landed on the desk beside Alec's right hand.

"Psssst!" said the tramp. "Water!"

Alec filled a paper cup and put a few drops on his finger. The tramp drank the drops eagerly. "Got anything to eat?" he asked.

7

Alec took out a cracker and crumbled it. The tiny tramp gobbled crumbs and stuffed more into his pockets. He peered at Alec's math paper. "What's that?" he asked. "Is it hard to do?"

"Math—yes, it's hard."

"Then why bother?"

"So when I grow up," Alec told him, "I won't have to float around on a dandelion begging for something to eat."

DORIS, THE BRONTOSAURUS

Doris, a brontosaurus, often exclaimed in despair, "I haven't a thing. I haven't a thing! I haven't a thing to wear."

One day, Doris received an invitation to a ball. "I can't possibly go," she cried. "I haven't a gown."

"Go," urged Doris's mother. "Wear something. Anything. Don't mope. Go."

The ball was only two days away, not enough time to stitch up a new gown. So, at the last minute, Doris chose a cloud to wear. The cloud was damp, grey, and quite plain. But it fit her so well, Doris felt like the belle of the ball— until that cloud began to rain.

This left poor Doris in a terrible muddle. Wherever she danced, her gown rained a puddle.

BLUE MONDAY

The horse awoke: Monday again. He sighed, and then he climbed into a tree. "Why are you trying to hide?" asked a girl who happened to be sitting in the same tree.

"I don't feel like working today."

"Why don't you just take your phone off the hook? Then you won't have to hide."

"I don't have a telephone," said the horse.

"Then why don't you just ignore your doorbell?"

"I don't have a doorbell," said the horse.

"What kind of work do you do?" asked the girl.

"I pull a buggy. All day long, the same old buggy."

"Why don't you just get in the buggy then, and take a ride yourself?" suggested the girl. The horse said he had no one to pull him. The girl said she would. So the horse got into the buggy and the girl pulled him around the park.

"All a person really needs is a change once in a while," said the horse with a contented smile.

WHY HARRY THE CAMEL CRIED

Harry was a camel. Children rode on him at the zoo. When they laughed, Harry was happy. But when they cried, Harry felt so upset he could scarcely walk.

"They decide I'm terrible before they get a chance to know me," Harry told Clara, the hippopotamus.

"Try smiling," suggested Clara.

The next time a whimpering girl was lifted aboard, Harry smiled. The child screamed. "What big teeth! He's going to eat me!" She was quickly carried away.

"Try humming," Clara told Harry.

When a little boy cried, Harry hummed. "He's grumbling and rumbling," the boy yelled. "Take me off!" Harry felt so upset, he had to lie down.

"You know what, Harry?" said Clara, "I'm out of ideas. You're on your own."

The next time a child cried, a large camel tear rolled down Harry's cheek. "Oh, look! He's crying!" the weeping boy said – and laughed. Harry had found the answer.

CHIPPIE'S MYSTERY

Chippie the Chipmunk had a new book, a mystery. He climbed into bed and began to read. The story was bloodcurdling.

Chippie reached under his mattress of leaves for some berries. He always stored food there so he could eat while reading in bed. But this night, not a single berry could be found.

"Who stole my berries?" he yelled.

"Not I," said the weasel.

"Not I," hooted the owl.

"Nor I," hissed the snake.

"Where exactly did you put the berries?" asked Chippie's wife. "Not, by any chance, in your jaws?"

Chippie's jaws did bulge suspiciously.

"Oh—yes," said Chippie.

"Aha! So you haven't been robbed," his wife pointed out. "All the while, the berries were right under your nose!"

11

THE KING'S GREAT DANE

The king was getting forgetful. He left things here and there. So his daughter gave him a present—a Great Dane. "He will fetch the things you've forgotten," she explained. "Great Danes have a fine reputation for fetching. Sometimes they travel as far as five miles to recover forgotten things."

One Wednesday morning, the King left his crown sitting on a rock beside a stream where he had been day-dreaming. So he sent his Dane to fetch the crown.

When the Dane reached the rock, he found not a crown, but a bullfrog. "Finders keepers," croaked the frog, who had hidden the crown. And he refused to give it back.

So the Dane took the frog to the King, and the King put it on his head. "But that's not your crown," his daughter reminded him.

"I know," whispered the King. "But I think my Great Dane is getting forgetful. He doesn't seem to remember what my crown looks like, and I wouldn't want to hurt his feelings by mentioning it."

12

THE MOUSE'S CHEESE

The mouse saw the falling snow.

"It's raining milk," she told herself. "I'll save it and make myself some cheese."

The mouse collected the snow in a bowl.

Soon the snow melted into water.

"I've been cheated!" she yelled at the sky. "Cheated by your crooked cow!"

THE GORILLA WITH GOOD MANNERS

The gorilla looked in the big standing mirror and smiled. A dark someone was smiling back. Dark, with fierce eyes and a fuzzy topnotch.

The gorilla looked around behind the mirror. The dark one was gone. Back to the front. There! The gorilla put his hand out to touch the dark someone. Flat. Cool. "Hmmmm," said the gorilla. He scratched himself. The dark someone scratched, too.

Then he sat down. The dark one in the mirror also sat. The gorilla stuck out his tongue. So did the other. "That's not nice," scolded the gorilla. "I don't want to play with you."

He got up in a huff and walked away.

14

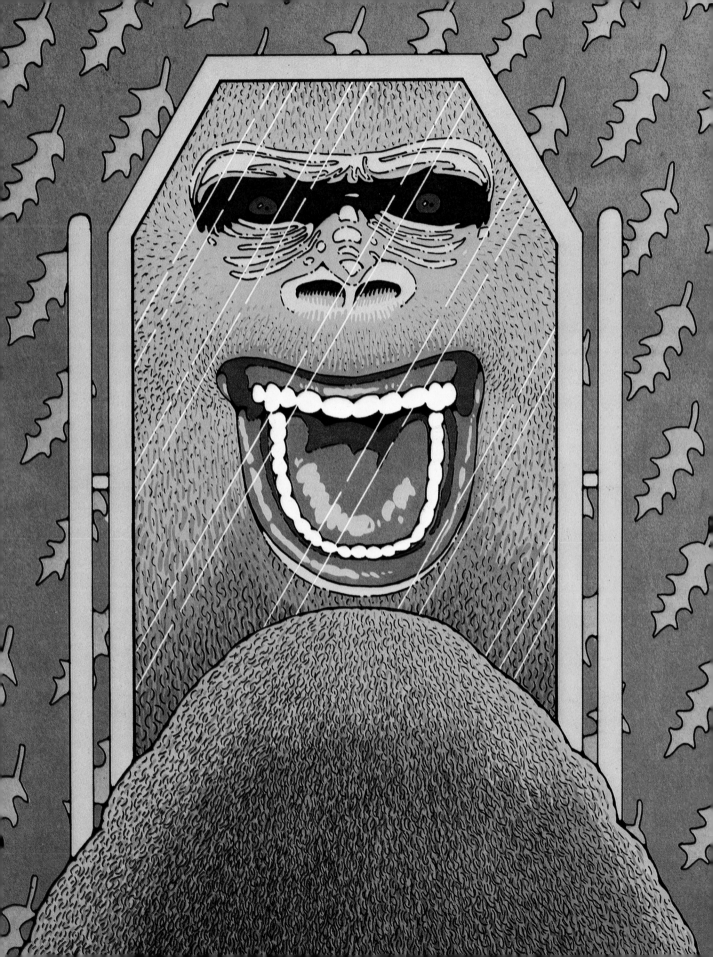

THE OLD GIANT TORTOISE

The old giant tortoise blinked his eyes. He could see that it was day.

He blinked again. Night. There were the beautiful moon and stars.

He moved his left foot an inch. That took all winter.

The old giant tortoise opened his mouth, caught a fly and swallowed it down. This little snack kept him busy all spring and summer.

"Time. What is time?" he thought unhurriedly. "A blink here, a blink there, a footprint in the sand, a fly."

Meanwhile, time continued on and on and on and on. "Next year," the old giant tortoise told himself as he yawned, "maybe I'll have lunch–if there's time. Why rush?"

15